The Story
of the
Plain Brown
Wren

Suzanne Anderson

LifeRich Publishing is a registered trademark of The Reader's Digest Association, Inc.

LifeRich Publishing books may be ordered through booksellers or by contacting:

LifeRich Publishing
1663 Liberty Drive
Bloomington, IN 47403
www.liferichpublishing.com
1 (844) 686-9607

Because of the dynamic nature of the Internet, any web addresses or links contained in
this book may have changed since publication and may no longer be valid. The views
expressed in this work are solely those of the author and do not necessarily reflect the views
of the publisher, and the publisher hereby disclaims any responsibility for them.

Any people depicted in stock imagery provided by Getty Images are models,
and such images are being used for illustrative purposes only.
Certain stock imagery © Getty Images.

ISBN: 978-1-4897-3051-0 (sc)
ISBN: 978-1-4897-3050-3 (e)
ISBN: 978-1-4897-3077-0 (hc)

Library of Congress Control Number: 2020916370

Printed in the United States of America.

LifeRich Publishing rev. date: 11/12/2020

On a bright, sunny day, The Nest birdie friends gathered on their favorite playground. Their dear friend Brother Eagle sometimes joined them, and they all hoped today would be one of those days. From her tree swing, Wren quietly watched and listened. Her friends were bragging and boasting about how extraordinary they were.

"Look at me!", proud Penguin declared, "I'm the only one whose wings are powerful flippers. I can swim like a fish!"

Peacock strutted around spreading her spectacular feathers out six feet in the air.   She blustered, "My magnificent blue, green and gold colors are the most beautiful of all."

Not to be outdone, Robin trilled, "You can hear my glorious singing from the time the sun comes up until it goes down at night."

Blue Jay screeched, "I have the loudest, most ferocious call of all. No one can beat me in scaring away danger."

Their words stung. Wren knew she was not exceptional
like her friends. Wren knew her talent was small.
Almost in a whisper, Wren said, "I can
bore a hole into a cactus."

Jeering and laughing the birds taunted Wren.
They exclaimed, "That's all you can do? You are
certainly not gifted and talented like us."

Becoming bored and hot, the birdie friends soon wished for a cooler place to play. They remembered a cave near the playground and headed off together to explore. The braggy birds were certain of their ability to handle the new adventure awaiting them in the cave.

Soon, however, the five feathery friends were hopelessly lost deep within the dark cave. The frightened birds remembered that no one knew where they were.

Looking up high in the cave, they saw a teeny tiny beam of light peeking through a teeny tiny hole. That ray of light seemed to be their only hope, but could they reach the small opening and squeeze through? They had been bragging and boasting about ways they were the brightest and the best, but could they save themselves?

Fearfully, Penguin uttered, "My flippers are perfect
for swimming, but not for flying. I can't save us."

Peacock fanned out her huge and impressive colors into the
darkness. "Oh, no," she said. "No one can see me, and with
these long feathers, I will never fit through that hole."

Then Robin sang out in her most beautiful voice,
"My music cannot rescue us," she said.

"I'm just too big and bulky and boisterous" said Blue
Jay sadly. "I cannot save myself or my friends"

One by one the frightened friends gave up hope
of being rescued. They were trapped.

Wren loved her unique and clever friends, even when
they boasted. She wished she could help.
Could she bore through that small hole?   Would
the plainest, quietest bird of all be able to
escape the cave and save her friends?

Timidly at first, she spread little wings
and began to fly up   up   up

toward the light.

Then Wren pecked and bored into the tiny opening, and slowly but surely squeezed and wriggled her way out. Once free, the happy little Wren flew off to find someone who could rescue her friends. When they were all safe and sound, the birdie friends gathered once again at The Nest playground.

Brother Eagle joined them and welcomed his little friends. "So, you've had quite an adventure", the wise leader said. Brother Eagle lovingly told the birdie friends that God designed every detail in His creation. He shared how God made each of us gifted and talented so we can love and serve others and follow Him.

He added, "When you mocked the plain, brown wren, you almost missed seeing what a masterpiece God created. Every one of us is a one of a kind, special, limited edition. Rather than being proud and boastful, we can celebrate our uniqueness knowing God has a plan for us."

One by one the little birds asked Wren to forgive them for belittling her. Remembering the joy of saving her friends, Wren quickly accepted their apology. Wren invited her thankful friends to their cool, refreshing bird bath to jump and splash and play together once again.

The Bible says in the book of I Corinthians that God does not like boasters, and tells us to be humble. Then, in Genesis, God says He created everything, and it was very good.

Verse References: Genesis 1:31

I Corinthians 1:31

The rich creative graphic design depicted in this scene is from the original artwork created by The Nest Christian Academy. A leafy, life-sized tree, imaginative bird characters and their bright birdhouses, and a playful birdbath decorate the lobby and classrooms at The Nest campus. The unique graphics depicted in this story also leap from the curriculum pages used by The Nest Preschool.

The joyful learning opportunities for children in the local Texas community should be shared. The message of redemption depicted in the birdbath represents God's offer of love and forgiveness for us all.

About the Author

Suzanne Anderson

Suzanne attended Bible seminary and has an undergraduate degree in nursing and a master's degree in marketing. A successful entrepreneur, she pioneered a unique healthcare business and consulted with other entrepreneurs for years prior to founding and serving as director of The Nest Christian Academy in Argyle, Texas.

Suzanne grew up on a steady dose of children's stories shared by her late mother, grandmother, and great-aunts. Creatively, through the eyes of The Nest original bird characters, Suzanne retells these stories from childhood memories. The stories are old, but the truths are evergreen.

Now a grandmother herself, it is her hope and prayer her stories are told and retold, and that they impact and influence the next generation. The stories are told in books and curriculum providing the basis for Christian education for young children. The stories tell the story of God's love and special Gift, His son Jesus. The most important story ever told is delightfully communicated to children in her books and biblically based, academically strong kindergarten prep preschool curriculum. In the words of Fanny Crosby circa 1880, "Tell me the story most precious. Write on my heart every word. Tell me the story of Jesus. Sweetest that ever was heard".